Also by Br

Meandering Through Time – Volume 1 (2020)
ISBN 978-1-913529-99-4

Meandering Through Time – Volume 2 (2021)
ISBN 978-1-913529-81-9

Meandering Through Time – Volume 3 (2023)
ISBN 978-1913529-06-2

MEANDERING THROUGH TIME

The Grey Granite Walls and the Lost Stories from Wales

Volume 4

by

Bruce Parry

Moyhill Publishing

Copyright © Bruce Parry 2024.
All Rights Reserved.

No part of this publication may be reproduced, stored in a retrieval system, or transmitted, in any form or by any means, electronic, mechanical, photocopying, recording, or otherwise, without the written prior permission of the author except for the use of brief quotations in a book review.

The moral right of the author has been asserted.

First Published in 2024 by Moyhill Publishing

ISBN 978-1-913529-24-6

A CIP catalogue record for this book
is available from the British Library.

Cover design and typesetting by *Moyhill* Publishing.

Contact below for ordering, information and interest
in my publications and work

bruceparrymeandering@gmail.com

Moyhill Publishing,
Unit 135393, PO Box 7169, Poole, BH15 9EL UK.

Dedication

This fourth book is dedicated to my children, Jason Karl Parry b. September1976, Lana Adele Parry (Baynton) b. October1978 and Gemma Lacey Parry (Evans) b. August 1986. I am very fortunate to have had three healthy children with my wife Lynda Barbara Parry (nee Norton). They have grown to be remarkable individuals in an ever changing world, indeed, producing grandchildren that have changed all of our lives in so many short years.

This book, mostly written by my late father, Emlyn Parry, travels through time from a world long gone, a world of childhood recollections and character observations from the tiny Welsh communities of North Wales in the 1930's and beyond.

This book is a sometimes sad but also a joyful recollection of inherent Welsh life, love and despair from an age long gone that my own children will never know, I hope they will read this in the future and learn from an almost lost history.

Bruce Parry.

Contents

Introduction 1
Rose 3
Watchman… 10
The Night Watchman 12
Sam James and Martha 14
Jane Pritchard 17
Mrs. Robetts, the voice 19
Di Gloom Evans 23
Johnny Tombstone Evans 26
Mrs Erskin 29
Rev John Owen Morgan 32
Nell Mary Parry 34
Meredeth Jones 37
Ellen Jones and Owen Hughes 40
Emrys Johns 43
Miss Beatrice Owen 46
Pobydd Edwards 52
Joyce Buxton 54
Little Miss. Foster, Miss. Howarth Jones,
Henry Hughes Davis and Mr. Tudor Aber ... 57
Morgan Roberts 61
Dick 'Donkey' Kelly 63
Cassie Owen 66
Talog 68
Gwilym and old Beth 71
The Quarry 74

Contents Cont'd…

Foreword –
  The Welsh Wizards and The Yellow Skipping Rope ... 77
The Welsh Wizards 79
The Yellow Skipping Rope 89
Black and Tan 97
The Valley 101

Introduction

Over the years, my late father wrote much about his childhood and adolescent years, with character observations and short stories from his memories and life in the small village of Penrhynside, Llandudno and surrounding area's in North Wales. This book and other stories within were inspired by meeting and talking to the Night Watchman and visiting his tiny hut on the hillside behind the village. These memories and stories were collected and later written down, and after his death in 1981, my late mother, June Parry, put an original book together with her own character drawings as a tribute to his observations and people in a time gone by, with all of its poetic licence, elaboration and by today's standards, perhaps some degree of political and social incorrectness of small Welsh communities characteristic of the times. This project was my parent's final artistic collaboration. I endeavour to posthumously re-launch this collection with additional stories and poetry left out previously with my own creative ability over forty five years on, father, mother and son…meandering through time together again.

The similarity of names, places and persons deceased or otherwise, is purely coincidental as part of the story telling process. My own contribution and editing to this work will hopefully move the creativity forward to a modern readership.

Rose

The paint was cracked and lifting along the edges of the sweet shop windows in a town where an age had passed…

Stacked with sweets as rosy as old Rose, who somehow smiled sherbet that fizzed and liquorice that shined, where childhood gathered on sunny lemonade and wet splashing in puddles days…

Thick glass jars looked out, half full, half alive with topsy turvy dolly mixtures and black jacks ready to jump as children jumped in playground days…

On foggy days, street lamps illuminated the speckled thick white air, but yellow tinged in a central aura, half lighting the sweet shop door and windows…

Old Rose, wrinkled and bright eyed, peeped out through ageing glass at the swirl of fog that was November again…

Opposite, the church spire pointed the town upwards with windows lit for the hopeful masses, who now stayed home behind warm brick with contented table lamps…

Nobody is ready for the quietness of fog, descending like a silent film without ending, all except old Rose, scarfed, gloved, hatted and leaving for home…

Keys turn in the shop lock that is worn to perfection, finding comfort in Rose's heavy coat pocket… rattling and escaping the chill of damp that seems to drift along the sooted terraces…

Walking along, Rose's head is full of chocolate soldiers and Angels that she has laid out on display that will hang on trees, cotton threaded for next month, wrapped in shining crinkly foil that will tempt…

Still child-like, Rose thought back to the winter of 47, it was white, white as sheet, silently settling on green and tile…

Huge flakes, floating down bouncing on noses and scarves, blowing along and tumbling towards street lamps and telegraph posts that stood defiant and half covered, 'crisp and starched' like staff nurses in an old hospital…

Rose smiled at the memory, but shivered as age chilled her bones, bones as white as the china doll that had sat by a small Christmas tree on draughty floorboards in that winter of hearth play to find warmth by the fire…

Home at last, the fog followed her through the front door as if wanting to stay for the night and chill her till dawn, Rose closed the door quickly to retain the little warmth within…

A ticking of clocks, one loud, one soft, found their way across the silence of the linoleum hall and living room speaking the language of time, well wound clocks in a house that had become timeless…

Rose reached for the matches to light the fire in the grate that had been laid criss cross to perfection that morning, whilst dawn chased away another night, revealing cold rooftops and birds fluffing their feathers on telephone wires that were ugly in daylight…

A large tea urn stood proud and well polished on a trolley in the kitchen, it was Rose's turn for the tea roster tonight down at the old theatre, where rehearsals were underway for this coming seasons pantomime…

Rose, a long standing member of the amateur theatre group waited patiently for her helper to arrive, Shirley, the very try hard actress and singer who had never been picked for one single part in any production but contended herself with the responsibility of supplying the biscuits…

Tonight, the trolley would have to be pushed through three foggy streets to the theatre, bumping and clattering through the silence of night, both Rose and Shirley waxing and waning over past productions and tea urn triumphs…after all, this tea urn was electric and admired by many for its somewhat modern thermostatic control…

Rose noticed the unusual cake tin that Shirley had placed next to the biscuit tins, mostly filled with emptied bags of broken biscuits that were always the best biscuits to buy in the new supermarkets… disputes at rehearsals had often broken out over the even amount of broken chocolate biscuits to the ratio of plain and ginger…Shirley felt that this biscuit phenomenon had become quite a responsibility whilst shopping…for broken bags of biscuits…

'What's with the cake tin Shirl, didn't know we supplied cakes as well these days?' 'It's for Emlyn Rose, that nice bloke who sleeps under the stage some nights, to be honest, he's not got two pennies to rub together, manager says he can stay over if he helps with the theatre, I've been making him cakes and sandwiches…!'

'You been down there eavesdropping Shirl?' 'He's a really clever bloke Rose, he's an amazingly good actor and singer, he writes and tells wonderful stories and he's been running the Repertory Group there, that's why the manager lets him stay under the stage, the manager says he'll be really famous one day.'

The tea trolley, complete with prize tea urn clatters to the side entrance of the theatre building, the fog is even thicker now, Rose coughs as she breathes in breathlessly from the effort, the quiet streets seem even quieter as people stay inside, the few cars that there are will certainly not be chancing these foggy conditions tonight…

Rose and Shirley moved the trolley inside, the smell of grease paint and warm air met the fog as they struggled through the door, the theatre had no tea urn, so this was a lifeline for stage and crew alike, if the theatre did have a tea urn, the amateur groups were not allowed to use it…!

Rose

    Once set up in the theatre kitchen area, Rose and Shirley sought out Emlyn, as usual, he was scribbling down stories on a make-shift desk under the stage, Shirley handed him the cake tin of goodies. 'Thank you, said Emlyn, your just in time to hear the beginning of my new stories from my childhood reflections, it all started with a poem I wrote long after meeting the Night Watchman on the mountain quarry behind my old village in Wales long, long ago.' Rose and Shirley sat down on some old costume trunks listening intently…and so the story begins… the thick fog outside swirled and fell to ground like a ghostly theatre curtain on a first night…

    All three, Rose, Shirley and Emlyn settled down, the story began…it started with a kite…'A kite is a wonderful thing, when I was a boy and the wind was high and showed a temper…I would tread my feet to my highest mountain. Right up high…standing alone in the screaming wind, my hair wild across my face. Sometimes…when the wind blew very hard, the tears would streak across my face like tiny jewels…but I didn't care, because I was happy with my kite.

    Holding tight to the long bending string as it quivered and pulled, I would run hard and fast along the sheep tracks. And oh! They were lovely days… those kite days, as my feet ran across the greenest green…under the bluest blue. And I shouted as loud as the wind through the tall crags…but no one could hear me; only the skylarks perhaps, as they darted from their nests when my running feet disturbed them, but I'm sure they understood I was happy…

Then, when the kite was high and far away, you had time to look down to see the grasses bending over…like tall thin ladies bowing after a special dance. And the yellow gorse, fern and bracken seemed to laugh and enjoy as the bustling wind pushed across their heads…to stop them doing what they wanted to do!

Over the cliff edge…beyond the quarry, there was the whipping green back sea (like a dragons back)…throwing the boats around as they bobbed and danced to all the tunes I knew…and the spray leapt high like chandeliers of mist through the bursting sun, then disappeared, as the wind conjured it away high in the sky. Then…I would look up again, and sometimes there were clouds.

Clouds in different shapes…they sailed across the sky. I would wipe them out suddenly, and shape them into all the pictures I wanted! The seagulls I would always see – as they swooped and hovered on the wildest wind…

They shrieked and cried around my kite, and I think they were happy too! And still looking up, I would pretend I was riding on my kite…so that I saw all the world below. From up there I could see all the pyramids…snake-charmers, the Indian nights, with people in veils and dressed in white…and the humped back camels moving lazily across a desert rise…

The world went around and around, as I ran my kite to the highest cloud…and the wind laughed and agreed with me, as we enjoyed these days. Once…I wondered if the wind had wiped all the stars away… but when night came, they were still there, like big diamonds on the black velvet sky.

But always…I ran fast across the heather tops… with all the laughing, crying and dancing things. I will never forget those wonderful kite days…the windy…blustering kite days, that sped…and dreamed me home to sleep. If ever the kite string breaks… don't cry too much, a kite belongs to the clouds.'

… 'It was an evening sunset, my kite had landed by the remote night watchman's rugged hut, and the church bells chimed across the sullen valley, chimes of my first poem.'

Thoughts of a Night Watchman,
North Wales 1930's…

Watchman…

As a boy I recall the watchman and his hut
Like a magnet I was drawn close to their side,
That stout wooden castle to hold him each night
Yet, I wondered why he felt no pride.

He'd wick trim his lamps, lay them in line
All grouped around and close by his side,
Filled with care, to last the long darkest night
Yet, I wondered why he felt no pride.

Strong brown hands, would place each one
Illuminating like stars, along a black roadside,
Like soldiers all in step and burning bright
Yet, I wondered why he felt no pride.

The coke fire chuckling, and all aglow
Tea can chattering and pipe by his side,
His eyes saw each dawn, whilst others in sleep
Yet, I wondered why he felt no pride.

His warmth of fire, which I loved to share
And longed to stay all night by his side,
To tell the others, I'd watched through the night
Yet, I wondered why he felt no pride.

Watchman…

He never feared the shape of night
Or eerie owl startling, when it cried,
He was so brave, thought I, as a boy
Yet, I wondered why he felt no pride.

If I stayed all night, I'd check his lamps
And build his fire, when he sighed,
Let others sleep, while we kept watch
Yet, I wondered why he felt no pride.

Each morning I awoke, and knew he was gone
Never once did he mention the dark world of night,
Moon secrets were his, and his alone
Yet, I wondered why he felt no pride.

The Night Watchman

Moses Jones, night watchman, qualified guardian of trenches, drains and holes that others dig, and graves before filled. Children call him 'Holy Moses' behind his back.

As Saturday night meets Sunday night in parcelled weeks throughout each year, he snuggles inside his wooden hut, tea-can at the ready, brazier topped high and glowing, pipe filled, and midnight two puffs away.

Wicks trimmed, red-coated lamps, winking, blinking, all in line on guard in dark and drenched earth, waiting for dawn to wash them out. Only the distant chimes of St. Mary's church, from the valley, will speak to him through starlight hours as they float over the mussel-bedded shores of Rhos.

Heavy shouldered black silhouetted Snowdonia range yawns away into a bilberry night, peeping at a sleepy sun as villagers settle and chimneys say goodnight.

Two hundred and eighty warm beating hearts snuggle down within ageless granite walls to dream or count the hours to Bible time. The Cross-Keys is closed, mopped up and dried, yet a lingering

The Night Watchman

perfumed malt mixture still drifts through the village, by-passing the chapel with caution, and sobers up on the salty lulling sea below.

The Night Watchman

Sam James and Martha

Sam James, the drinker, known by most as 'The Container', has consumed his usual fourteen pints, and now staggers along the road…and off it, singing the only song he knows, 'Drink to me only', belting out of his frothy bubbling throat. Then stops, to make his regular call beneath Martha Gibbons' bad-tempered window, relieving himself against her prize hollyhocks, clinging desperately against the wall.

'Open up, Martha bach caried, and give us a kiss…I've got my peppermints tonight" he calls. Sash cord window scrapes open to let in the night air, an angered Martha peers down with arrows of abuse. 'I've heard of your peppermints, go home and redeem yourself meddwyn mul' (drunken mule) she barks and snaps the window closed on her calico nightdress room and dreams of a carefree stolen passionate moment she shared with Sam long ago behind her snug granite walls.

Sam James raises his cap, forgets to button his trousers, laughs, and staggers on into the waiting night. A drinker of vast quantity, swears to boasting the barrel alone can only hold more than himself. Out of favour with half the village for his pastimes,

Sam James and Martha

while the other half hoard a secret jealousy. Found once, lying asleep, half-buried in mountain snow, on being revived his frozen lips spluttered out, 'Are they open yet?' He sleeps five nights in a bed of a weekday and a rocking chair on Saturdays.

So he rocks snoring and smiling, dreaming of barrel-made galleons on a sea made of beer. His voice nightmares through to the small hours, 'Fill them up, boy'o, fill them up.' Tears roll down his scarlet cheeks as distant voices haunt him, 'Time gentlemen please.' His Annie upstairs sobs and cries into her pillow, 'Time is a taker, not a giver!'

Jane Pritchard

The chapter-less night sets the watchman's thoughts, as a foxing moon glides and bounces over the mountain peaks. It spills its silver threads over Scarborough House and Jane Pritchard. Oh, so different, Jane Pritchard, she's the oldest and the nicest of them all. Calls the house 'Scarborough' because her husband came from there and prided herself to have taught him Welsh hymns before he died.

'She's the oldest and the nicest of them all.' Won't have electricity in her house…still burns the yellow flickering paraffin lamps and cooks on the black polished grate…had six fires there already and still says, 'It's safer than thunder.' Still buys the English newspaper since her husband died, and can't read a word of English herself.

Twice a week, Jane Pritchard pilgrims to St. Mary's churchyard, flowers in one hand, and a package of English newspapers tucked beneath her arm. With divine regularity, places the flowers and newspapers on the grave, duty bound to Arthur who always liked to read the newspapers undisturbed.

'She's the oldest and nicest of them all.' Snuggled down, child-like, widowed, dreams of Jerusalem,

Meandering Through Time – Vol 4

Jane Prichard

birthdays, Christmas cards and hymn books. And so she sleeps each night, wedding-ringed for life to her Arthur and hopeful eternity, and only one year from ninety.

'She's the oldest and nicest of them all.'

Mrs. Robetts, the voice

The watchman shuffles the brazier with a twisted poker wand making sparks fly. Dancing shreds of demon fire sprites are blown and point the way to ivy-cottaged bed of Pen-y-Bryn, where snores Mrs. Robetts 'the voice'.

Round as a melon, pink faced as a carnation, her sleep as compulsory as she is, a worker of some repute – Mrs. Night and Day', so the children say. Competes with the bees humming, her endless sawing of logs through summer, and qualifies to feed her open grate from first leaves that fall to first bright daffodil that droops its head.

Remarkably voiced…tone less, but what a voice! It rolls down the hill, screaming for the attention of her grown sons from the top granite wall like Hercules. Bouncing down the village to fields beyond, muffling the school bell toll. All those whose ears are fractured with its sound exclaim 'Cryn Duw.' (Good God).

Still the voice booms above the screeching gulls, 'Alfie…Tommy.' The only female voice they and all men fear. The only voice that never reached the village choir, invited or otherwise. Small, as she is big, her husband trembles at her call and has been heard to utter two words, 'Do, oes cariad'. (yes, dear).

Dogs respond by wondering why kennels have no doors, dreaming of bones and St. Francis, ears muffled down and tails tucked in. Lumbago once a year does not silence her voice, wintergreen vapour-laden breath hurls itself from the bedroom to the household below, still thundering on!

No one dared to step on her white scrubbed doorstep – if they did, it was at their peril. Everyone who called jumped the step, those that were acquainted. It had been told that an insurance man once dared to defile the Holy white stone. Mrs. Robetts, all fifteen stone of her, lifted the man bodily and wedged him in the dustbin. He never did it a second time; in fact, he never called again.

'Two coffins she'll need', says Dick the post, and went on, 'One for her and one for her voice'. 'You're dead right there', replied Albert road sweeper, switching off his deaf aid whenever he spied her coming. He smartly turns the other way, swiftly sweeping two toffee papers, his first industrious effort since working for the council some twenty years ago.

So, there she lays, feet cosy in grey woollen socks in bed deep thoughts, she turns and snores like a volcano.

The Voice, Mrs Robetts

Albert Roadsweeper

Di Gloom Evans

A spiritual moon hovered over the deserted quarry basin, below, which nestled Aderyn Copse. The night watchman observed its mystic light etch out 'Respose House', only funeral parlour of the district. Exclusively owned by twin brothers, Di and Johnny Evans, and their father before them. Born in a single act of birth, but divided in appearance as those well known comics, 'Laurel and Hardy' shown at the threepenny picture house.

The skinny smaller of the two, referred in name as Di 'Gloom', money lender, debt collector and undertaker. Sallow of complexion, habitually rubbing his bony hands together. Always tape measure at the ready and a morbid interest in the sick.

'Touting for custom' Dick Post ruefully announced to Albert road sweeper, 'Yes, always in anticipation of the next customer' replied Albert. 'He will never be short of them, that is certain' concluded Dick Post. 'Very true, very true, a box is waiting for all' concluded Albert, shaking his head solemnly.

Di 'Gloom', a mean man by nature, kept his wife Eira in piety and obedience. Clothed in a coat and dresses acquired thirty years previously when first

Meandering Through Time – Vol 4

Di Gloom Evans

Di Gloom Evans

married. Yet he himself, dressed always in an impeccable black frock coat, crepe trimmed top hat. When walking before the cortège, placing one foot in front of the other, reminding one of a tightrope performer.

Certain in his monopoly over everyone, who he knew would eventually bring business to his door like a waiting spider, sure of its prey. Secretive in his affairs, but all suspected his accumulated wealth, not kept in the Post Office, or a bank, he was a man who trusted neither, but he had some deep hiding place known only to himself.

It was said, that on dark nights, if you passed his lighted blind shadowed window, you could see his hunched figure busily intent over his books and money boxes. Money boxes secured with chains and padlocks. If you listened carefully, you could hear the chink of coins, and his mumbles of counting distinctly.

Meanwhile, his wife Eira, would be kept stitching into the late night, muslins, satins and silks, making linings for the coffins till her fingers became sore and her back ached. A beautiful job she made of them too, a real artist at work.

Never an extra penny of housekeeping did Di 'Gloom' afford her. Every penny Eira had was duly accounted for and recorded in Friday night's account book. Ritually, Di 'Gloom' inspected scrupulously each week, not even a farthing escaped his seagull eye. So intent on his book keeping, he never noticed his wife's other accomplishments, Eira had a lover, her gloomy husbands' twin brother Johnny.

Johnny Tombstone Evans

Johnny 'Tombstone' so called, a portly jovial man of philosophising countenance. Whether an impressive or simple stone monument for commemoration, or cemetery purposes, Johnny 'Tombstone' was the man for you.

He sculpted cherubs, Angels, or simple memorial markers for permanence. His large skilled hands caressed huge stone slabs, moulding and chiselling them into delicate, intricate forms of masonry art. Known for his political outbursts, maker of rhymes for all occasions, chiselling out immortal verse for remembrance of the dead, reminding the living that their turn was coming.

A spare time builder of walls around houses and fields, a skill envied by most sheep farmers who were unable to enclose their own pastures. Charging three pence for inside 'toppling' per span build, and four pence for outer wall 'toppling'. Difference in price he concluded, inside wall 'toppling' less work in distance than outside wall 'toppling'.

When it came to wall 'toppling', Johnny 'Tombstone' was the best, he knew every flint stone by shape and feel. Lodging one stone upon another,

Johnny Tombstone Evans

balanced with the same mathematical precision as the ancient Egyptians applied when constructing the Great Pyramids.

Never needed to marry, his secret arrangement with Eira sufficed his manly appetites, sharing artistic pursuits and bodily harmony. Spent the rest of his free time downing beer at the pub like a fast running stream. His brother, disapproved of this wasted occupation and money, and told him so on every occasion.

Johnny 'Tombstone' paid no heed, his drinking only came to a halt when his money ran out. After hours, he could be seen tip toeing unsteadily along the village street, holding out the linings of his empty pockets between forefinger and thumb, reminding one of a comic ballet dancer, calling to the moon, 'No pockets in shrouds Di bach, no indeed – no pockets in shrouds'.

So as Di 'Gloom' occupies his time deep into the night counting his fortune with glee, his brother Johnny 'Tombstone' and Eira creep away to keep themselves warm behind the grey granite walls.

Mrs Erskin

Shadows deepen and cloak about the watchman, his witch-like fingers point and curl about Bella Vista. Crumbling grey shadowed broken Bella Vista with black garbed Mrs. Erskin within, wears a veil and seldom ventures out.

A village personage, unsolved, descended, arrived, and the story ends. Neither letter nor visitor passes between barbed wire holly berry trees, or the tall shrouded yew trees, or wade through broad nettle beds all enjoying a full span of growth, knitted close with hand cutting grasses high as the dark window sills. Trailing ivy had finished its work long since.

Her tall gaunt figure shadows across dimly lit windows each night, her darting small bright eyes peep behind lace curtains, darned with cobweb spider hours throughout each day.

Children have fear of the house, never to trespass beyond the grey crumbling walls. The deep shadowed Bella Vista and the strange shadowed Mrs. Erskin, who they believe is a giant rat by night because from within her secret walls comes scratching, scratching, always scratching.

The Virginia creeper, clinging, climbing to the topmost cold chimney, tired itself out by climbing down again. As its leaves turn green to yellow, and then blood red, the grey rats gnaw and collect within the moss-cushioned porch, hold their councils. Local cats with hair on end take the long way home, while the village lock their doors and snuggle down behind the grey granite walls.

Mrs Erskin

Mrs Erskin

Rev John Owen Morgan

When the moon points shadows over the poplar trees, the watchman sees the chapel house, rightful owner and abode of the minister, Mr. John Owen Morgan. Collector of people, guide, comforter, and keep them-in-order. His huge hands and stretched arms almost engulf the surrounding mountains with his presence. His white collar evokes smiles and nods in plenty for the believers. Mumblings, blushing and look the other way for strays from his fold.

He can handle a funeral congregation with the same warmth and sincerity as he does the white laced weddings. Of the young…he tells the old; 'Meet them half-way.' Of the old…he tells the young; 'They're nearly home, meet them all the way.'

His warm sense of reality shines through, when, after a funeral, a daughter cried to him; 'They made a mistake on the coffin, Mr. Morgan…my mother was eighty…not eighty-one', she protested. He looked into the daughters eyes deeply and replied kindly, 'Does it matter very much, my dear, what the calendar reads when the Lord calls?'

His warmth, humour and wit stand cliff-top high over the village, as the endless miles, in stretching years, grow larger in his gallery. Mr. John Owen Morgan, minister, sleeps with his book full of two hundred and eighty warm beating hearts, in their rightful order, as he dreams of his oak carved pulpit, behind his grey granite walls.

His once Sunday voice cried out; 'If you can't afford some collection on the plate, don't sit back and hide behind the heaters, come down front and warm yourself with a bit of listening.

John Owen Morgan

Nell Mary Parry

Two walls past the chapel, the moon picks out Rhos-View, where Nell Mary Parry sleeps. The singer, contralto…and, oh…a velvet voice that was. Every Eisteddfod has heard her sing, rosettes line her walls and a glass cabinet, in profusion of rainbow colours.

Her voice drifted from within her walls in winter, and from her summertime garden. Soft as an ostrich feather, deep as a melting lake, pure as a mountain stream. The village respects her voice more than her person. Women halted over their Monday wash, as her voice bubbled and drifted over the dolly tubs. An opera house hardly a stone's throw away for her, but she stayed, stayed to watch the children grow up and the oak trees age.

Small, slightly rounded, she faced the adjudicator at the annual Eisteddfod, with poise, stance and dignity, hands clasped gently before her as if in prayer, eyes to the gallery, her silver notes extracting sighs from the audience.

Adjudicators ears were smoothed in contentment, all pencils trained for ninety nine of a hundred, and her modest melody rose richly to match the music of

Nell Mary Parry

heaven. And so she sleeps, smiles, dreams of mountains, streams, children, La Boheme and Tosca, sung sweet behind her grey granite walls.

Meredeth Jones

A pebble singing stream turned itself into a silver ribbon and slipped past the watchman's feet, as the moon pocketed behind a cloud to take a nap. Then the water wound its way past Dylis Lodge where Meredith Jones, choir master extraordinary, slept between the sheets clad in silken nightshirt and newly knitted nightcap…

Voice silver – threaded as the stream that flowed past his wall. Well known figure, sharp and tall in his dancing tail suit, leader of choir and operatics, and leader of women to his bed.

His conquests sit side by side in choir and operatic rehearsals, smiling shyly, coyly, and seductively wriggling, while his wife, Awyddus, wistful and yearning, pretends not to notice. Baton in flow, he marks the beats and surveys the ladies before him.

He smiles in satisfaction, as daughters resemble mothers…and himself, the offspring of his orchestrations. Mistresses and sons mirror each other, another reminder of his own busy youth!

Crotchet jumping lines, minds and bodies in composition behind the cricket hut, or on mountain hidden gorse beds, or deep inside wild woodland hides to play stolen love making scores. Mary Williams, newcomer, the try hard soprano sits in the chorus, her unwelcome voice drowned out with surrounding talent. But Mary sleeps with Meredeth Jones and the other women hate her, but Meredeth Jones likes her figure.

Awyddus watches him sleep from her own lonely bed, stares at the ceiling and wonders why she married him. Once he called her dainty as a firefly, now age has made her brittle as a dried-up fern. Their granite walls grow greyer and their snugness has become her imprisonment.

Meredeth Jones

Meredeth Jones

Ellen Jones and Owen Hughes

Across the lane, established rock – firm as the granite walls, is Mrs. Ellen Rynn Jones newspaper shop. Wiry, thin as a bamboo stick, she bounces off her heels as if wearing two bed springs.

Lassoed and married little Davy Rynn Jones thirty years ago. Widowed ten years later, now left to count his money and hold the purse strings. Thin as a telegraph pole, the children of the village call her 'Visibility Nil.' Like a hopping bean, she jumps around the village, she is the beginner of all days.

Polishes her brass knocker and letterbox each midnight, with mouse like silence. Children chalk on her plate glass window, 'Rise and Shine.' Papers are delivered and finished before dawn nods its head. Up and sorted before the cock crows, fire lit, toast in stomach and away…blindfolded by the darkness. Buttoned boots brushing shrubs, disturbing the fresh laid snow, breaking mirrored puddles, while the inhabitants are still in their dreams behind the granite walls.

Mumbling to herself at each letterbox, 'Mentioned in dispatches, that's me, if time keeping was the issue.' Finger tips frozen, whistling 'Onward Christian

Ellen Jones & Owen Hughes

Soldiers'. The bundles of papers fold silent speeches and sales of the week listed on page nine.

Her endurance of hard winters and warm summers include those pretending smiles and 'I'll pay you next week Mrs. Jones!'

She goes her way, with half an ounce of black twist tobacco in her pocket, in case she meets Owen Hughes the poacher. Her silence appreciated, for a half ounce of twist in exchange for a nice plump hare never went amiss. Collecting more news than she took from gossipy Owen, whose eyes never close till the moon slides abed.

Emrys Johns

Emrys Johns, of broad countenance, with florid bewhiskered face, presided over the 'All sorts shop' of the village. A plenitude of everything, glass-jarred dolly mixtures, suck through liquorice sherbet and lucky dips, nothing over a penny.

Bundles of wood for the fire, kept tidy with a twist of wire, dominoes, dolls houses, elastic by the yard…for those that need it. Comic books, shaving leathers, cut-throat razors, brushes, yo-yo's and wind riding kites.

Sticky toffee apples and gobstoppers, hymn books, and bloomers under the counter, silk or cotton for summer and fleecy-lined with a pocket, for winter. Back and front press studs, elastic arm bands and fly-papers. A sign above the door:-

'SHOES TO MEND BY ARRANGEMENT.'

Jolly and stolid, round as a tower, booms a big band drum on carnival days and holiday days… weddings by appointment. A leader of men in his gold braid and letter-box-red uniform, and no brass band in all the land had such a man.

His deep rolling voice, matching the power of his drum, drowned all efforts of a rowdy football crowd. His 'Bread of Heaven' rendering echoed around the mountains and down the pass in thunderous roar. But, beyond this station, he spent his days behind the counter, his size and weight eventually wearing a backwards and forwards groove in the heaving floor boards over the years. Meanwhile, his busy fly-like wife flitted from counter to fixture, avoiding the sticky fly-papers set to trap all fast moving objects.

The hanging fly-papers collected everything, the variety was astounding. Fluff from Ellen Jones' woolly hat, one of old Bens bootlaces, layers of moths and flies, candle-grease and chewing gum, and even a bit of unsuspecting toupee. Shutters closed, lights out by nine at night, Emrys Johns and his wife Blodwyn, lie in a snow-white double bed, side by side, like mountain and mahomet, within the grey granite walls.

Emrys Johns

Miss Beatrice Owen

A ghostly, lazy, half sleeping moon observes the watchman and the pyramid gardens of Ruthin House high on Bron Hill. Miss. Beatrice Owen, wealthy woman, collection of money complete, but her collection of shells from the shore goes on. It would be well to remember that, in giving orders, she was ladder top in the village. Invariably received and carried out promptly, heard to say with regularity; 'I'll give orders from the grave, if I wish it!'

To quote Ivor Williams, breeder of Christmas geese and local butcher; 'She doesn't play that piano of hers, the ivories duck when they see her hands coming.' Such large hands and flap fingers like Ivor's plump, strung-up pork sausages.

Each Sunday morning after chapel, a sermon, four hymns, her favourite 'Those In Peril On The Sea', returns home, latch-keys her door, then out again with a large wicker basket, leaving sizzling roast lamb with mint sauce mixed in the Arga awaiting for her return.

With great haste, she makes her regular excursion down to the lonely, curving, white pebbled beach. Close knitted hat in winter, and her straw

Miss Beatrice Owen

Meandering Through Time – Vol 4

hat trimmed with bird of paradise and flowers in summer.

Cautiously, as if tip-toeing a bed of porcelain, hands carefully L-shaped, she begins choosing and picking the best dressed sea shells, with dignity, between the forefinger and thumb, reminding one of a jeweller at the height of his profession. Miss. Beatrice Owen is not unlucky, she collects and fills to the brim her basket. Struggling with her weighty finds, returns home, tips them out with great care at the bottom of her garden.

Result of her tireless work, the collection is prominent. One observes the gradual disappearance of the blackberry and gooseberry bushes. The pile devours the fence at the end of the garden and swallows the garden shed, all now a mound of shells. Over the years, colours, shapes and sizes huddle together like a large tomb.

So it goes on, the graceful picking, the gentle tipping, whilst the sea in partnership with her, shuffles more up with each relentless moving tide. From sea to the garden they come, separated and washed clean of the mackintosh seaweed, misfitted and naked, bigamously married to Hill top Ruthin House.

Unknown are her reasons, but a collection of hopeful, accurate, pinpointed opinions serve as a topic of village conversations. 'Albert road sweeper' speaks with guaranteed confidence; 'Its transplanting the Irish Sea, that's what it is…and keep your eyes open when she starts with buckets.' Mrs. Osborne of New Lodge, quoting from gossip and fictitious law books, snaps through her false teeth; 'Living on stolen property if you want my opinion.' Of course, nobody did want her opinion. 'Ron Watkins', gnome-like, leather tanned skin and frisky fisherman, eater and sleeper of Lloyd George and no other politics, parliaments his eighty years experience; 'Building another Suez, shouldn't wonder?' 'Little Mrs. Berry, who takes in borders for a living and very patriotic, asks; 'How will the English holiday makers get sea level in summer with all those holes she digs on the beach?'

Miss. Beatrice Owen sits late into the night writing her last will and testament, for the presence of Mr. J. Hollingsworth, solicitor; 'I, Beatrice Owen, spinster of this parish, request after my death the removal of sea shells with appropriate care. Not on Sunday, but remove them from my property and return them to their rightful owner, the sea. To be transferred by Messrs. Griffiths and Sons, removal contractors of Neptune Square.'

Still under the white shrouded moon they shine, unclaimed, like a great collection of Neapolitan antiques, surrounded by competing granite walls.

Meandering Through Time – Vol 4

Ron Watkins and Dick The Post

Miss Beatrice Owen

Ivor Williams

Pobydd Edwards

The moon sharpened the outline of Tawny Cottage which stood out like a slice of cheese on approach up the hill. Cut sharply in two, front part balanced on the village main road, while the other half tended to drop down out of sight under the rock face ledge. Contents of which housed several families and a shop under the same roof, sharing the hours of day, and sleeping separate at night.

Pobydd Edwards had the shop part for his bakery. Throughout the nights, summer and winter alike, his ovens were well stocked and rarely ever went out. As the fires roared away, the smell of fresh bread and cake bakes spread over the mountains and down to the bay.

Dough boxes, all in line, tall and shelved, his large sinewy hands slapped and punched the never ending mounds, mixing pastry and dough into mouth watering morsels. If one could not afford to buy, you could inhale and smell freely and gaze hungrily, a window of jam tarts, seed cakes, rock buns and stacks of baps that heaped from a floured floor to the ceiling, like a great hill in a climbing prelude.

Pobydd Edwards

Many a lad felt Pobbyd's oversized rolling pin crash down on his lower regions when he nicked a bap from the middle of the well balanced pile, which made the baps collapse and roll out of the door and sometimes down the hill. There was no wastage though, each bap retrieved, dusted off with flour, and held in residence for consumption as 'A pennyworth of stales.'

Pobydd Edwards

Joyce Buxton

A communicating cottage door separated a flat from the bakery. Here, the only English family of the village snuggled behind Welsh granite walls. A family that could contain a mystery, educated above most, and stood high in keeping their home like a new pin.

Mr. and Mrs. Buxton and their daughter, Joyce, came from London where the King and Queen lived, and so they held a certain important place in the lives behind granite walls. Mrs. Emma Buxton kept much to herself, tall, unnaturally fair with dark roots, posh hats, veils, bejewelled and always gloved. In winter, sported her envious fox fur shoulders, and in summer, her chiffon figure floated in and out of the village shops.

Joyce Buxton, her daughter, not a striking beauty, had elegance, and was a dancing teacher in Tegwyn. This, itself, had much standing because days are hard and work scarce, and no one of the village could afford dancing lessons. From their flat, the sound of music came constantly, for they owned a wind-up trumpeted gramophone, which led all to believe that they only had one record, 'The March of the Tin Soldier'; nothing else was ever heard.

Joyce Buxton

On fine days, village children sat on the wall opposite and watched with wonder, Joyce cavorting with the grace of a hockey stick, all legs and arms, batting an unseen ball. To them, her performance compared favourably with the Pierrot's on the pier. In spite of her protruding teeth, she did have a lovely smile.

Mr. Buxton was a dapper little man, dressed in immaculate pressed suit and spotted 'dickie bow tie.' Never without a silver - topped cane on Sunday, and wore putties on his legs throughout the week, a reminder of the Great War. Had a habit of wrinkling his nose up and down like a busy woodland rabbit.

The only time Mr. and Mrs. Buxton went out together was to vote on voting day. They slept in separate thoughts, cosy and private, within the grey granite walls.

Little Miss. Foster, Miss. Howarth Jones, Henry Hughes Davis and Mr. Tudor Aber

The watchman stirs his thoughts and stares at the paling moon slipping into dawns first light. Over the woodlands, wild peacocks and hens scream like calling cats. A mile away, the school will later wake with school bell call…and prayers before and after. Small and brown, with creamy white gabled fronts, carved and grooved on one side 'Merced a Babanod', girls and babies, and on the other side 'Bachgyn', boys.

It stands glued to the asphalted playground, held down by a heavy quarry-slated roof keeping it in place, to ensure mountain winds or lashing rain will not sweep the building away. Soon the children will come running, eager for the halfpenny cup of Horlicks, the elixir of existence, to quell a biting hunger shared by most. So from Treview Terrace and beyond, the teachers wake to take their little charges.

Little Miss. Foster, dark, smiling, with a crooked nose and a large bun at the back of her head. Miss.

Howarth Jones, a large lusty woman with auburn hair, bespectacled and amiable. Miss. Simms, the English teacher, all the way from Liverpool – tweedy sports, hair fixed close in earphone-like plaits. Played golf in broad flat shoes, shiny buckles and flapping leather tongues, strode like a man from heather clump to heather clump.

Henry Hughes Davis, a large, flabby, puffing, blowing man, charged about the school like a Snowdonia mountain train. All eyes riveted on this red cheeked expanse of a man, who blew out like a whale in temper. Emotionally charged, his abusive words raged down on his pupils in storms and tempest. It was not unknown, at these inflamed words, for his false teeth to dislodge themselves, drop from his mouth and lay still chattering all by themselves on a desk or floor!

Mr. Tudor Aber, headmaster, tall, thin and shiny bald, fidgets with his large gold watch chain, stretched from waistcoat pocket to waistcoat pocket. He moved between the desks with spatted feet, eagle eyes and a thin stinging cane tucked beneath his arm.

Little Miss. Foster, Miss. Howarth Jones, Henry Hughes Davis and Mr. Tudor Aber

Henry Hughes Davis

Mr Tudor Aber

Morgan Roberts

Children spent happy days revelling in play, combined with noise and mischief until Morgan Roberts, the village 'bobby', threw his large shadow across their merriment.

A fat man with red face, fully moustached, and small darting eyes which had the unfortunate knack of seeing back, front and sides all at the same time.

The large uniformed body strode over the hills, down the valleys and along the lanes, raising fear in all he passed. That fear rose to terror when he raised his only companion, a great knobbly walking stick held fast in his grip, and could shatter a school slate at six paces.

He lived in the top terrace above the village, overlooking everyone and everything. Although strong walled, his cottage could hardly contain the rumblings and swaying of his huge frame.

When pubs are closed, his uncertain steps rolled his barrel of a body steeped in beer, home to his dear little eight stone wife, Kitty, who has learned over the years to suffer his brawling abuses, while his son and daughter vanished into the woodwork until their father recovered.

A man, who, however much beer he consumed, was entirely wide awake all hours of the week.

Morgan Roberts

Dick 'Donkey' Kelly

There was no better way to get the boys' blood circling than an encounter with Rhiannon Kelly, only daughter amid seven boys of Dick 'Donkey' Kelly. Both father and daughter well endowed with nature's bodily achievements.

The large family lived in a shack at the bottom of Dysgl field, tumbledown, but water and windproofed, and shared the field with ten donkeys. Unexpectedly, the donkeys were cared for with great

Dick 'Donkey' Kelly

regularity, a safeguard income over the summer months for visitors on the sands.

Mrs. Kelly, so large that she overflowed two chairs, plodded from shack to shed, feeding the scrappy hens and de-licing their numerous dogs, doing all the work that got done, and then contented herself with the comfort of a gin bottle!

Dick 'Donkey' had Romani Irish blood, a shock of dark curly hair and large round blue eyes, indeed, a handsome man. He contented himself serving the holiday population on the summer beaches with donkey rides, and lonely females up on Cragfel Copse in more ways than one!

The children often stalked this gigolo through the long grass, spied on him from hidden tree branches, as he set to work on his latest conquest; he was not named 'Dick Donkey' for nothing.

Like father, like daughter, Rhiannon was well developed beyond her years, and was not ashamed to flaunt herself and unravel the mysteries of growing up and how babies are made. Her school blouse always too small with a button missing, and she wobbled in certain parts deliciously. The children sang a rhyme to shame her forward ways;

> 'Here comes naughty Rhiannon Kelly,
> Boys, have you got a penny?
> She will show her belly,
> *Only cost a penny.*'

Dick 'Donkey' Kelly

Rhiannon Kelly

While Mrs. Kelly sleeps in gin-filled dreams, 'Dick Donkey' contemplates his next conquest, and Rhiannon counts her growing heap of pennies, surrounded by the Grey Granite walls.

Cassie Owen

With light of day, the Watchman picks his way between the grey granite walls. His watching over for the night, he moves down the village towards his cottage 'Bedwyr', to sleep away his daytime hours and make his own dreams with his Gwenn.

Of the children, he knew them all; little Cassie Owen, nicest dressed of them all, kept in quietness and unmixing by her mother. Her father was never seen or talked about, his absence most noticeable.

Milly Wyn at the post office has never had or seen a widow's pension book in Cassie's mother's name, yet not one penny did she owe anyone.

Once a week, a posh car, driven by a uniformed toffee-nosed chauffeur, called for Cassie, opened the door for her and treated her like a real lady. Dressed in her best pink serge dress, hair ribbons to match, she Sat in the back of the car like a Queen.

Destination unknown, destination untold, but winter and summer, the posh car called at Rhos Villa without interruption over the years…taking Cassie on her secret journey.

Cassie Owen

Cassie Owen

Talog

Talog, jaunty by name and by nature, small and thin for his nine years, trod the mile and a quarter to school each day, wearing the same gaberdine mac and cap, year in, year out, and lived with his father alone. His four sisters had gone to live in English foreign parts and married respectably. His elder brother lost in the vast continents of army life.

Grate unfed, larder low, mostly empty all year round, and a pot of bacon ribs all and every day, when a pennyworth of gas would allow.

Suffering a bleak cold winter, Talog, with all good intentions, trudged two miles in the biting snow with determination, to bring a log, which seemed as big as himself, all the way home. He had decided the empty fire grate would shine with heart-warming heat, and give his ageing father some comfort for once.

On arriving home, almost exhausted, but over the moon with his triumphant efforts, proudly displayed his roped find. His father, less than enthusiastic, stood at the door perplexed!

'For the fire tada.' (Dad)

The old man scratched his head;

'Too big for the grate, boyo,' he muttered.

Talog

'We can saw it up,' said the boy, eyes shining with good feelings.

'But we havn't got a saw,' replied his father, dampening the moment of joy

That cold night, Talog climbed the stairs, snuggled down in threadbare sheets, and cried himself to sleep in disappointment.

Long years afterwards, the log remained in the garden beside the Poplar tree, a milestone of years, until it fell to dust and the wind scattered it back to where it had come from…

Gwilym and old Beth

Dawn yawns over Bradwen Hill and hesitates over Owl Cottage, the smallest and last house of the village, where Gwilym sleeps lightly behind his granite walls. He sleeps almost awake because of his watching over the long-tailed sheep.

Almost eighty years a shepherd, winter and summer, over the hills with faithful Beth, the last dog in a long line of dogs, his sole companions ever at his heels.

It is known that on one particular snowy day, old Gwilym, in his eighty fifth year, awoke to find Beth unmoving…so still. Wrapping the dog in an old blanket, he trudged the weary three miles, dog in arms, to the vet at Tegwyn, all the way crooning to the dog, 'soon have thee well lass', stroking her soft black head.

The vet, a kindly man, took the bundle from Gwilym's arms, cold and wet with snow, looked at the man, slightly bent, furrowed with years, respectful, cap in hand waiting hopefully. 'She'll be all right sir, won't she? She's all I've got now', said Gwilym, and went on; 'I can pay you, I've a whole shilling saved up for Beth.' The vet placed a chair.

'Sit down Gwilym,' he coaxed, kindly and gently. 'I'm sorry Gwilym, but Beth is dead, been dead some while.' The old man's face crumpled and tears welled into his eyes. 'I thought it was strange she did not wake me today.' The vet placed a consoling hand on his shoulder. 'She was well passed her time, a great old lady,' trying to ease the man's grief.

Gwilym was at a loss. He wiped his eyes and sniffed. 'Think I got a cold coming,' he excused, then, gathering his thoughts, went on; 'You will take care of her, won't you?' 'Of course I will,' reassured the vet. 'She were a good friend, but she weren't a thoroughbred you know,' somehow excusing the situation. Gwilym placed the shilling on the table, and touched the old dogs head lovingly.

'Will that be enough to take care of her properly?' He asked. 'More than enough, I must give you some change.' He took the shilling and crossed to the drawer and dropped it in, retrieved four pennies and handed them to the man.

'There, take the tram home Gwilym, it's such a cold long walk home.' Gwilym still sleeps lightly, sometimes smiling as he dreams of Beth's happy barking, behind the old grey walls.

And so the village greets each day and each night with shoulders above the sea, locked between the mountains, kept safe by the ageless grey granite walls.

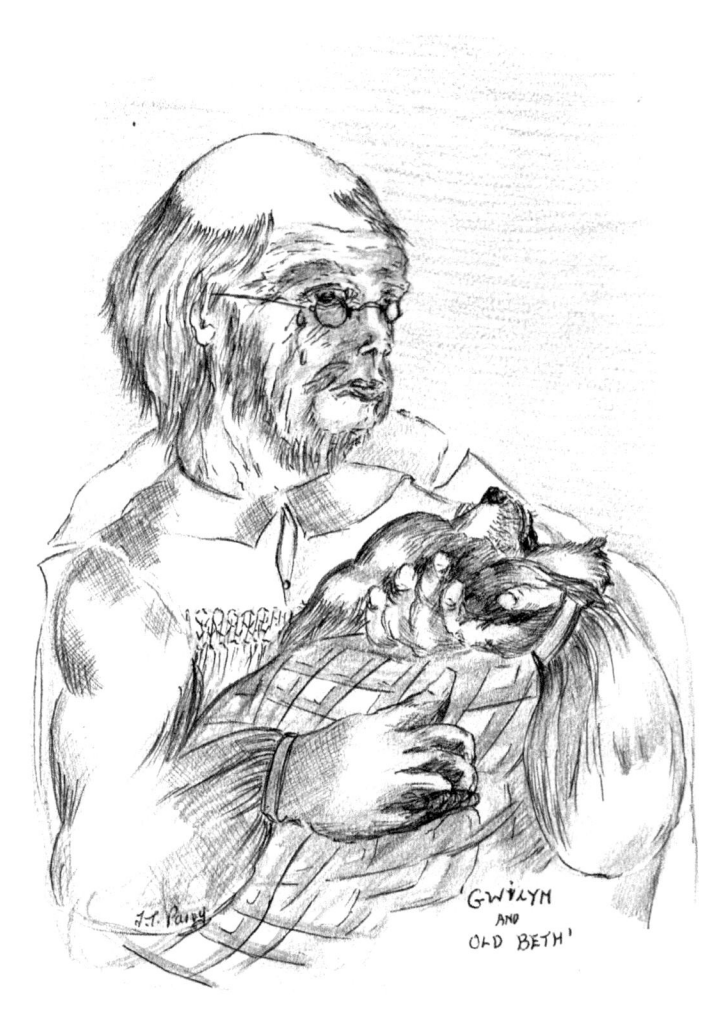

Gwilym & Old Beth

The Quarry

The Quarry is dead like the grave…

An age has passed,
since men did leave unfinished work to die…

Nature pushes back its weeds and grasses, to
frame the abyss, like a knitted garment strong…

The gorse and thistle
are the land owners once more…

Screaming gulls take the place of heavy studded
boots, and their nests secure the places,
where man rammed the powder…

Resting huts are broken, their rusty roofs rattling
to the wind as if awaiting men's return…

The wages office is still and dead,
where man reached out their hands for bread.

Winter and summer still come and go,
where ghosts of men walk to and fro…

Hear only the thunder roll,
where noise of blasting made the hole…

Wire ropes on the rock face lie,
handled by men who did leave them to die…

The Quarry

The ebb tide unwanted,
where ships nosed in to take the load…

Only crumb searching robin,
will leave his print in winter snow.

The Quarry is dead like the grave,
the remnants are their monuments…

The granite tomb is strong, but men have gone…

The book is closed,
they reached only a middle chapter…

The wheels of trolleys will turn no more…
that carried the stone, from incline to shore.

The Night Watchman

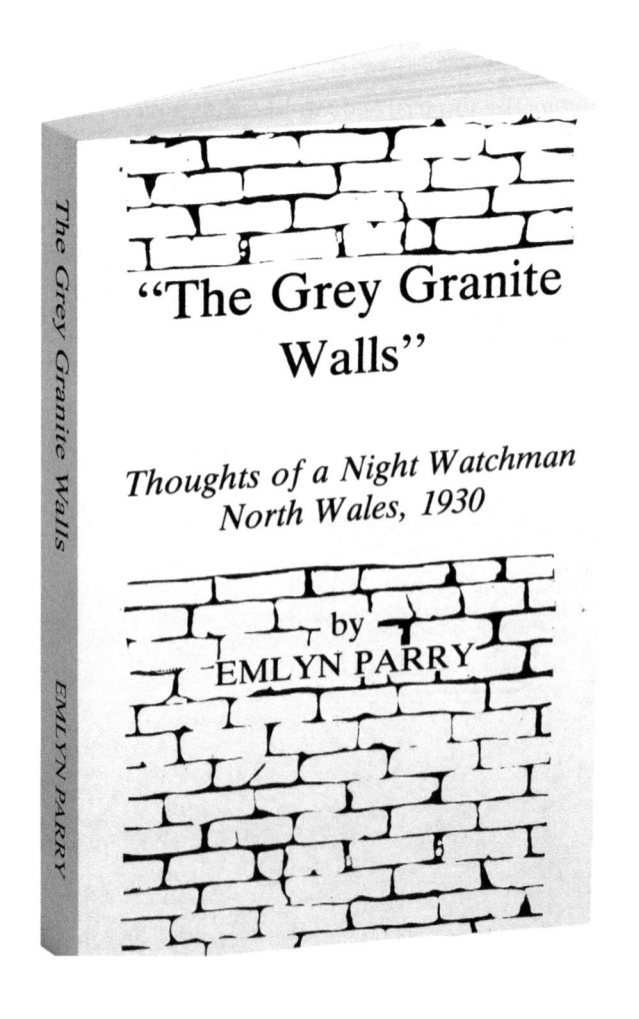

"The Grey Granite Walls"

*Thoughts of a Night Watchman
North Wales, 1930*

by
EMLYN PARRY

Foreword – The Welsh Wizards and The Yellow Skipping Rope

Continuing from '*The Grey Granite Walls, Thoughts of a Night Watchman, North Wales, the 1930's*', the late Emlyn Parry continued to write short stories and poetry based on life in the small village community of Penrhynside and Llandudno. It was as late as the 1990's that my late mother June Parry finally typed out these continuing stories and completed new artwork before she died in 2006.

Once again, I have re-edited and re-structured the new artwork to enable these works to continue on into the future, perhaps before the world forgets how different life was during the 1930's and 40's. I think that my late father was a true storyteller, these later works bring much pathos and sadness to the stories, and once again revolve around inanimate objects, a special watch in The Welsh Wizards and a skipping rope in The Yellow Skipping Rope. The theme revolving around inanimate objects which tell stories, continues throughout The Grey Granite Walls in many chapters. I hope you will enjoy these continuing new stories and artworks….

Bruce Parry.
December 2016.

The Welsh Wizards

The funeral was over, grave diggers had finished and straightened their respective hats, picked up their shovels and departed the cemetery, helped on their way by a cold blustering wind. Even the Reverend Morgan had shown more anxiety on his face…from the sharp weather rather than grief, and hurried away.

Albert was dead, laying beneath new dug earth, a floral wreath from the village folk, and a wild holly spray from his only two life long friends who stood by his lonely graveside.

Largest of the lone mourners, Jos Owen, all seventeen stone of rounded proportions, draped in a large button less overcoat, held together by safety pins from the neck down. His huge puffing torso propped up by thick corduroy trousers and hob-nailed boots…which struck sparks on the cobbled lanes. Each boot laced with different coloured string, suitably disguised with black boot polish. Jovial of face, heavily moustached under a worn out cloth cap. Because of his mountainous size, the children of the village nicknamed him 'Owen Snowdon' behind his back.

His companion, Johnny Muffler, a puny eight stone in weight, wrapped in an ankle hugging mackintosh faded with time. Always hatless, his bald head smooth to reflective polishing. His thin neck highlighted by a long woollen muffler, (scarf), wound several times about it, which earned him the name of Johnny Muffler, his real name lost in time.

With Albert, all three had been friends for years, they had walked, talked, complaining, sulking, gossiping and laughing and sinking pints at the Cross Keys. Villagers naming them affectionately '*The three wizards*' and '*the know all's*', forever convinced they were right about every subject under the sun. Even foretelling the future with knowing nods over seasoned years, now, their friendship was severed permanently.

Jos Owen flayed his great arms across his chest to revive chilled limbs, remarking… 'Well, you're on your way Albert old pal…even though you said you'd out live us…but you didn't did you?' with trembling triumph in his voice.

'You're dead right there, poor forecast by Albert, one time when he was dead wrong'…Johnny Muffler observed his unfortunate words of finality.

'Well, it's put an end to his showing off now' observed Jos, 'And his bragging!' His bellowing voice almost lost in the persistent lament of the north wind, 'You took the words out of my mouth Jos, at times, he did get above himself…always a bit of a show off. Take those posh bow ties…exhibitions on their

Albert, Deceased

Jos Owens

The Welsh Wizards

Johnny Muffler

own...and his gold watch, always flaunting them in front of women,' Johnny Muffler answered peevishly.

'Yes, always thought himself a bit of a ladies man' Josh remarked, 'That trilby hat...always raised it, especially to young lassies...copying film stars... remember how he bragged about meeting Laurel and Hardy, did you believe him Johnny?' 'Always made me wonder, but in honesty, he did play piano for silent pictures at the Regent picture house' he reminded his friend.

Laurel & Hardy

Albert had been the only Englishman in a Welsh village but for the Buxton's. He arrived many years ago, no one recalls why or when, most speculated he had secrets, some shady scandal, he never mentioned family but was never shy about his connections with

The Welsh Wizards

films. Albert, was into the 'talkies' when they arrived, but his two friends argued they would never last. All who knew him had to admit that at one time he had good connections, because he dressed well and was a polished gentleman.

Yet, he hadn't quarried the granite or slate alongside others? …still having hands the texture of a pianist. After work, he changed into a black suit, white shirt and spotted bow tie, and was very adept in teaching the piano ivories to obey his moving fingers, especially in the pub where ale flowed freely, and Jos and Johnny shared liquid proceeds showered upon all three.

Fitting together like jigsaw puzzle pieces, the three shared long strolls, purposely distant, missing meals that sometimes were not there. Political arguments they would cross swords over during winter nights under gaslight lamps, or by the night watchman's coke fire that they happened upon…now he was gone and a chapter closed.

Jos Owen gave a great wintry cough, it seemed to weigh on him as much as the loss and regret he was feeling. Johnny shifted uncertainly, leaving large imprints from his boots in the muddy earth.

Jos picked up the conversation, 'He didn't fool me with that baccy (tobacco) trick neither…I was on to his two tins…remember? One with a bit of baccy in the corner for our benefit, so pretending to be broke and not share…sly, his other full tin hid in his back pocket…he were crafty…had a mean streak', they nodded in agreement. Johnny Muffler moved to the head of the grave, almost tripping over his scarf…twice, in the attempt, muttering 'And that trilby hat…raising it for the ladies. I know the preacher does it, he has to keep up respectability, him wearing a dog collar…pulls them in for Sunday chapel.'

They both looked down at their missing link, the holly wreath suddenly slipped down the mound of earth lifted by the wind, the two leapt back three paces, 'Think the dead can hear?' Johnny Muffler whispered startled. 'Never speak ill of the dead' shuddered Jos, 'Even if he's well down six feet, more things in heaven…,' he broke off as if making excuses and resumed, 'But he did have good manners…can't never fault them.'

A cascade of sleety rain swirled about the pair, bounced along the cemetery walls before escaping through the iron gates. 'Think we ought to be going, soon be getting dark', Johnny drew his muffler (scarf) closer and they moved off reluctantly. 'So long Albert old mate' Johnny said quietly, 'Nice knowing you' Jos added.

The wind cut into their faces, sleet stung and mingled with tears that they tried to hide, as they stumbled through the shrouded cemetery and out through the gates as evening closed the day, as death closes all living things.

'We shall miss him, even though he was a show off…remember that snuff box lark…only on the tram mind…he never took a pinch at any other place' decided Jos, 'Said it was for his catarrh, 'How come he only had catarrh on the tram?' asked Johnny, 'Well, you know what he was like, always had to have an audience, and the tram was a kind of audience, least ways, captive until the next stop' reminded Jos.

'True, playing some fancy film tune count in… remember his cocked little finger? Some performance' concluded Johnny. 'Talking of performances' Jos reminded, 'I remember how we once had a go at trying his snuff, you tipped half of the tin on the floor, soon cleared the tram passengers…they all started sneezing, it got up everybody's nose.'

Both friends set off laughing at the recollection, 'He called you a man with the delicacy of a hippopotamus…you sneezed so loud, it resulted in spraying the windows on the opposite side of the tram bringing folk to their feet in alarm!' 'I wasn't the only fool' retorted Johnny, 'You bloody swallowed the stuff, the noises that exploded from your throat sounded like a pack of terriers after the fox.'

Arriving at their cottages, laughter subsided into silence, recalling many farewells at the end of each day. Albert always pulling his watch out eyeing the time, 'See you in the morning…goodnight gentlemen', he always referred to them as gentlemen. Jos and Johnny mumbled a familiar 'See you tomorrow', they departed to their respective abodes. This night was unfriendly, unforgiving, departing in a choked silence, wrapped in their own thoughts, aware time was ebbing away alone in their rooms.

Both found their pipes empty laying in their pockets, both wiping running eyes, blaming the wind for tears. Jos Owens large mitted hand clutched the silver snuff box, caressing the smooth metal. A stones throw away, Johnny Muffler removed his scarf from his cenotaph neck, revealing a bright dickie bow tie, he tapped Albert's pocket watch, held it to his ear, it ticked continuously.

Inscribed on the back of the watch was an engraving, '*To friendship always L & H 1920*' (*Laurel & Hardy*). Things would never be quite the same again.

The Yellow Skipping Rope

It was a white peppermint Christmas-eve night, snowflakes had finished their fall and lay married beneath self made eiderdowns. From behind parted clouds, a roaming moon let in the frosted silent light. Above the bay on iced mountain top, the bell tower of St. Trillo distantly managed it's last chime, almost shivering and glad to retreat until a longer count.

At the end of the village, woodland had surrendered, holding high its white gauntlet branches, halted still in striped frozen statue waiting for summer revels. Beneath the ground, moles lie sleeping, duck ponds are glass covered with decayed embedded rushes camouflaged, standing like a hundred shining swords.

Beyond, snow was holding hands from field to field, bulging hedgerows veined out the white sheeted world, the holly bush playing Christmas games with her scarlet beads. Glittering chandelier night, so hushed, even the tom cats had given up their slinking on freezing granite walls, now lying, purred and dreamy-eyed in front of good luck and merry Christmas fires.

Children have snowballed into sleeping dreams, riding giant reindeer locked in white bearded red hooded thoughts. Chimneys squeeze out skyward smoke trails marking a guide for the sleigh. Cold slated and warmed houses have taken over from the six hymnless chapels.

It is only Mrs. Price's shop that spills out the flooding new electric light, putting candles and oil lamps to shame, as its brilliance hits the hard packed street of snow. The framed glass window, tinsel trimmed, paper chained and holly bunched, with coloured fairy lights on a string, look down on cotton wool bobbles neatly glued together for snow, between last year's and this year's collection of toys.

It is a remarkable shop, a wonderful shop, glass jarred dolly mixtures, liquorice, sherbet suck throughs, shared shelves and boxes with bundles of firewood, dominoes, elastic by the yard, warm gloves and toffee apples.

Although the shop was closed, Mrs. Price darted from counter to counter, adding up on paper… ha'penth of this and ha'penth of that, while her husband snoozed in the back room.

Tub shaped eyes, closed, his uncut moustache twitching in a marionette dance by a log roaring fire. His musical snoring, in five seconds bursts, told of his contented dreaming…of two reared chickens… now oven clad…who only yesterday, were unaware that they were only one day away from his watch chain stomach.

The Yellow Skipping Rope

Mr. Wittle and Myfanwy at toyshop window

Outside the shop window, Myfanwy stands with her nose pressed hard against the magic lantern scene. The child uses her breath in heavy puffs against the frosted glass, huffing and with her worn out sleeves brushing away the misty patches to get a clearer view of within. Though the biting frost crept through her school jacket, settling on her blue gloveless fingers, Myfanwy was unaware.

Excitement and urgency blotted out the cold, shared only by the bright rolling moon. Her wide eyes roamed around the cavern of light, this way and that, but returning to the centre each time settling covertly whilst the night moved on.

Myfanwy had not heard the shuffle of Mr. Whittles feet as he drew close to her, and observed her with saddening interest. He loved children and in return, the children of the village adored the large portly man, with his never ending bag of sweets and kindness. His heart warming with chestnut fires on this cold Christmas Eve, he spoke softly…

'What may I ask, is Myfanwy doing, gazing here alone on such a cold freezing night, especially Christmas Eve…the shop is closed.' The child did not turn her head to look at him, she knew him so well, 'I was just looking at the yellow skipping rope…see the wooden handles…bright as buttercups, and silver bells like St. Trillo's Church' she answered.

'It is indeed the pride of Mrs. Price's window, in its bold red box.' He withdrew the accustomed sweet bag from his coat pocket, touched her gently, 'Have a

The Yellow Skipping Rope

humbug, it will warm you through.' Myfanwy took it gratefully, but her gaze returned back to the window, 'There, 'tis a handsome thing' she sighed, Mr. Whittle looked down at her over his upturned collar.

'Toys are funny things really Myfanwy, sometimes we want something so bad, and when we have it, we discard it without regret.' 'I was only looking' Myfanwy replied.

'Let us sit and look together', he drew up two discarded wooden boxes, brushed away the layered snow, unwrapped his muffler (scarf), laid it across the boxes, and they both sat down facing the illuminated window sitting in their icy comfort, as if to witness a game of mid-summer cricket, Mr. Whittle observed…

'See to the right Myfanwy, on topmost shelf, a interesting character, namely Bobo the clown. A remarkable trickster, somersaulting over the bar, landing on his feet, and the cap bangs from his trousers pockets. A toy to be used winter or summer, what do you say to that?' 'He is most clever Mr. Whittle, and my brother would love him, but I prefer the skipping rope.'

'Of course' said Mr. Whittle, 'It's a choice one must make, and a right to decide, but looking at things geographically, skipping is a summer game.' 'I wish it were summer forever' she sighed, shivering. Opening his coat, he drew her small form within, to keep out the icy night, and exclaimed, 'Now there's a lovely thing for you Myfanwy, a doll', he pointed to the flaxen haired beauty poised on the second shelf. 'With ribbons and shoes that come off, and if tipped slightly, will say 'Mama.' 'Truly a beautiful doll to take, even to bed. It has a unique feature, dressed in silks, and a face that will never grow old.'

'She is a beauty, but I fear she would be put out, and unhappy to ride in a 'soap box' pram', confided the girl. Mr. Whittle rubbed his chin with some thought, and considered… 'I have it…there's a fine present', he pointed to a miniature xylophone. 'An instrument of great pleasure, relative of the pianoforte. It too has the faint distant sound of St. Trillo's bells.'

'Music is not easy for me, I do not like music lessons in school', she pouted at the thought. 'I'd much rather roam the mountains with a skipping rope, hopping from turf to turf along the sheep trails.'

Imbrued to the bitter night, Mr. Whittle charted the conversation over the farmyard toys, past the dolls house, painting and crayoning his words over books and various toys…marching through tin soldiers, fairy dolls, jigsaws, crackers and candles.

The conversation ran down, Mr. Whittle rose to his feet and stamped them to let the warmth circulate throughout his cold body. Mrs.Price nodded at them, she was waiting to put the lights out and scuttle off to the warmer back room.

'I must be going now' Myfanwy said, almost apologetically, 'Thank you for talking with me, it was

The Yellow Skipping Rope

nice to pretend.' 'I believe if the good Lord himself offered you one of those twinkling stars up there…,' he pointed to the sky, 'I am of the opinion, you would still choose the yellow skipping rope.'

Myfanwy laughed and turned for the last time towards the window, 'I must be off…thank you Mr, Whittle and a merry Christmas to you', and began to move away. 'Wait, don't go yet', Mr. Whittle wrapped on the shop window sharply, Mrs. Price looked up, frantically he pointed to the door, 'We're closed' she called from within, 'open up woman, it's Christmas Eve' he shouted.

Tut, tut, tutting she came to the door, its dull toneless bell rang out over the quiet village, and Mr. Whittle entered the shop, almost dragging Myfanwy behind him. 'The skipping rope woman', he thrust the money into her hands. With impatience, Mrs. Price removed the red box and placed it in Mr. Whittles hands. As they left the shop, he sighed with satisfaction as the bolts shot home from behind the door, the bright window suddenly became blind and dark.

Above, the lighted stars monitored over the white rooftops and watched silently as he gave Myfanwy the box. 'For me?' Her eyes outshone the moonlit icicles pointing down from leaking gutters.

Myfanwy took out the bell tinkling rope and let the box slide noiselessly to the ground, lost in wonder, she left Mr. Whittle silent and standing alone to the chimes of St. Trillo.

'Be careful Myfanwy…be careful how you use it…'

Meandering Through Time – Vol 4

He stood smiling sadly, as he watched her tread the village road. A brilliant shaft of moonlight pierced the darkness and spotlighted Myfanwy and the callipers on both her legs…

Myfanwy holding the skipping rope

Black and Tan

At this age, how confident, but how reflective of times past, drifting back to my Welsh grandmothers house with it's dark curtains and stifled walls, steaming coal filled Arga stove that was almost built with the house, coal dust and slack coveted and hauled from a local quarry by night, bucketed and hoarded in a safe bunker behind the cheese, wedge shaped cottage that pointed to a moon as the night travelled through until dawn crowed.

I watch intensely as she pours her black and tan beers into a Wedgewood pattern cup with no handle, chipped and stained, a pale ale and a dark stout, two bottles to last the nights pall, nicotine stained fingers that roll her tobacco, now shaking, both hands lift this sacred chalice, her gaze is fixed in solemn comfort, smoke drifts from a roll up, the first of many that will fill an oyster shell ashtray by lamp lit bedtime and clock winding.

Saturday was the most important day, both the Cross Keys and off licence are closed on bible Sunday, this will mean two bottles of each beer must be procured on Saturday before 10.00 pm, to last through until Monday opening time, the urgency of this Saturday quest and purchase cannot be underestimated, the execution of Sundays black and tan will, as usual, be imbibed behind closed curtains.

My childhood observations tell me that the narrow street outside will never change, it is only my thoughts that will change in later years, it's pavements will take rain and snow many thousands of times before my adolescent return, where I will stand and know these walls and pavements and lives that wore them thin and shiny over time.

Below the village, the distant tram tolls up Penrhyn hill, vivid through the trees, it's clanging bell and faithful tracks gleam from rainfall that early morning, it stops mournfully to collect it's next load of long mac regulars, almost relieved it had arrived at the hilltop halt at Penrhynside, it will dutifully return here to offload the tired and coming home. As a child from a distance, there is a kind of sacred solace watching this huge object loading and unloading the tall, the thin, the large, and the clattering of shoes on metal chequer plate, it clangs into the distance.

The public toilets at the tram stop are almost built into the hillside of solid rock, I stand and wonder how they dug and chipped away into solid granite to provide this remote facility, a different way of thinking perhaps? My grandmother cleaned these toilets for many years, dawn and dusk, as an income through the hard times and as part of the house rental agreement, when work was truly scarce, rain or shine, duty bound, but never on closed up' Bible Sunday.

Charles and Mary (nee Williams) Parry at Trelawny Cottage, Penrhynside, Llandudno, 1950.

Her cottage was the end one of three, built on rock that would never move, opposite, were the higher up posh houses with gates, larger windows and it was said, better people with education and proper tied back curtains. As a child, you had to look up at those houses, built on higher granite, much like imaginary castles with local royalty, but the wealthy would pass away as quickly as the lower people to the same funeral parlour, 'There are no pockets in shrouds' many said, and the graveyard will always be over populated.

But whispered scandal still abounds in chapel and local shops, how my grandmother left home, husband and six children, for seven years, to go into service to feed and clothe the family in those hardest of times during the 1930's. It was said, that every time granddad hung his trousers on the end of the bed, another child was conceived…more pregnancy, more mouths to feed, she escaped to another world.

Sending money home each week from a mystery house and town, she being a remarkable pastry chef to the gold plated and well heeled in a place that was never revealed or talked about. The money came, the larder was filled and the children grew with each other and with their father alone. The years passed and the whispers became softer as hunger took it's toll as the quarries closed one by one.

It was the end of a chapter…

The Valley

From polished desks,
a brush has washed the canvas bare…

Thoughtless, hurriedly,
it swept aside my yesterday.

Now a sky invites windowed towering pillars…
where once trees gossiped through their lazy days.

Tall swaying trees…
that rented out a summer song…
to sweeping down of hills,
with breasts of corn and glowing mustard fields.

So far they reached,
my eyes never matched their distant wave…

Down they swept,
through hedgerows full of summer…

Unrolling ploughed up fields,
beneath hovering impatient crows.

Long quilted patches,
where weasels darted on sloping hidden banks,
near hawthorn bush, dressed in woollen tufts…
where sheep had ventured near.

Thread stemmed harebells, rang dating a breeze…
jigged to grated beat of grasshoppers in song.

The valley, where rabbits held their court, and
skylarks raced blue skies above the weathered gorse.

Nose down hedgehogs,
grumbling through a muddling ditch…
as rhythmic tails of cows…drummed away the flies.

Vanished the hay time smell…
lost the blackberry walks…
gone porcupine fall of chestnut time,
where squirrels leapt the bough.

Hushed forever, the crowing cock,
that pierced each dawn…near thatch-roofed snug,
dipped in trellis climb and summer rose.

Buried deep a shallow stream,
that daily fed its thirsty banks…then raced on…
under drooping skirts of willow.

Now, I gaze on bustling wild domains,
at concrete walks of shapeless display…

Hold down my beds of nettle,
which sailed the morning mists,
torn asunder my spiders crochet lace…
who's silver threads tied the sun.

Oh, this crying day,
that sent the melting hills to grave…

What careless tip of pen…
that signed this sudden death.

Emlyn Parry
1978.

Bruce Parry
2024.